A Bug on a Bar-Room Wall

A Bug on a Bar-Room Wall

A Bug on a Bar-Room Wall

A Bug on a Bar-Room Wall

A BUG ON A BAR-ROOM WALL

A Bug on a Bar-Room Wall

A bug on a Bar-Room Wall

An Earwig falls for a Cockroach in a neighborhood bar.

Library of Congress Cataloging-in-Publication Data
McGee, Willie.
    A Bug on a Bar-Room Wall : an Earwig falls for a Cockroach in a neighborhood
    bar / Willie McGee
    ISBN 978-0-6151-4532-7

FIRST EDITION

10 9 8 7 6 5 4 3 2 1

A Bug on a Bar-Room Wall

Acknowledgement

This novel could not have been brought to your shaky little fingers without the superb technical guidance of my brilliant son, Kevin McGee. Additional support was brought forth from my patient bride, Polly, my four best friends, (They know who they are), my five hundred eleven pals, and my two thousand thirteen acquaintances.

W. McGee

A Bug on a Bar-Room Wall

Chapter One
An Earwig Gets A Life

"Earline"

It was a dark and dewy evening in South Clairemont, in the first week of January, as the pediatrician was summoned to the Smith household. The news was good. Maternity was in progress there in the dank janitorial closet at Mesa Distributing Company a few klicks north of San Diego proper.

There, snugly nestled in a damp nine-pound floor mop, lay the entire roe-system of earwigs, bursting forth into a teeming mass of seven siblings: three female earwigs and four of the other. There had, of course, been many other generations to this family tree. There was the eldest, Melvin, followed by brothers Matthew, Mark and Luke and the three little wigletts, Kathy, Cathy and *Earline.*

Earline, the baby, was christened after her great uncle Earl, who had served two tours of duty infesting Wine-sap apples from Wenatchee, Washington and asparagus from the San Joaquin Valley of Central California, while on duty in diesel submarines in the Pacific Ocean.

The very week that she came into this world, Earline had a strong sense of wanderlust. Early on she chose to take up residence in a travatan colored Miller Genuine Draft box, with twenty-three adjacent condominiums. Her mother, Dina, admonished her to document her travels and trials in some sort of a journal. Uncle Earl thought that she was "just as cute as a bug." Earline had no inkling that her mother Dina, and Uncle Earl had a little action going on in the deep sink.

Earline had chosen a musky condominium. It was suitably dark and damp. She enjoyed the pleasant aroma of moist cardboard, hops, malt, barley and freshly milled pulp from Tacoma. Her favorite aroma, however, was the poignant, acrid air of newly cut Douglas fir from the great stands near Bend, Oregon, of which her pallet was constructed.

The Mesa Distributing Company teamsters had finished loading their great, white, *Mack* delivery trucks and were about to embark on their daily routes with their delivery cycles. They had downed their morning Red Bull, and had reviewed in detail just how on earth the Buffalo Bills could again represent the American Football Conference. The dominant Dallas Cowboys and their Teflon-haired coach, Jimmie Johnson had once again dispatched the Bills in Bowl Number XXVII. Little did anyone know that *that* was to be his last outing with the "boys." (This was considered astonishing, what with his track record and all).

A Bug on a Bar-Room Wall

The next most absurd event would be for the San Diego team to some day enter the Super Bowl fraternity. *Fat chance.*

Her comfort was suddenly interrupted as she felt a slight gravitational pull. She fretted. She had never felt this way before. Earline cried out to her neighbors, wondering where she was going, but evoked no replies. Her confusion and terror were substantial. She clenched each of her eyes tightly and snapped her forceps. Her sphincter constricted tightly as she began to feel genuine fear for the first time in her small memory. The awkward feeling and the incredibly new noises caused her to wonder if she was indeed in danger. She wondered what was going to happen to her and her future and how in the world she was ever going to find Mama and Great uncle Earl.

The drone of the big 6/71 Diesel engine in the great, white *Mack* truck and the high-pitched whine of the supercharger were quite enough to keep her hunkered in the confusing maze of her condominium. Together they rumbled south on Interstate Fifteen to an uncertain dark fate, somewhere near North Park in central San Diego.

It was a typical blustery day in late January as the Mesa Distributing trailer rig pulled up in front of a cocktail lounge on University Avenue at Richmond. Once again, Earline felt the effects of gravity as her condo was snatched up and lowered to a waiting dolly. It was her first weightless experience. The whole cargo was bustled through puddles, over potholes and curbs into a vast refrigerated room, where her condo was stacked atop dozens of clones.

A Bug on a Bar-Room Wall

The Teamster, Bob, then had to go into the bar to locate the owner, who had always been on a C.O.D. basis, often not being allowed to pay by check. Earline was unknowingly about to learn about this nether-world of the bar business (or Insurgency 101). Earline never saw Bob again.

She felt a little more secure in the turbid darkness of the walk-in cooler, though she noticed that she was living in a more frigid, more densely populated neighborhood than she was accustomed to. The architecture differed vastly. There were many colors, Colonial Navajo White, Avante garde Silver Bullet, post-impressionist Bud Lite, and English Tudor Red Dog. There was even a four-day-old platter of hard, greenish cheese, (or maybe it was just good meat). There was a lot of non-alcoholic beer and some cheap wine, in case the Gas Lamp crowd showed up.

The earwiglett rather enjoyed the change, though the melting pot syndrome made her a trifle ill at ease. Earline was not certain how to react to the changes. She was somewhat ambivalent about this Ellis Island feeling. Though she was delighted to be rid of the constant din and cacophony of traveling by truck-trailer rig, she still longed to enjoy peace and serenity. At this juncture of her short life, Earline made a decision.

In her journal, Earline noted on that very night, "It is the second day of February, Groundhog's Day. I am going to make a change in my life. I am going to move out of my condominium. I am surrounded by riff-raff. I am going to take up residence in a more temperate climate, perhaps Santee".

A Bug on a Bar-Room Wall

Early the next morning, as her condominium complex was being gently hauled into a receiving area within the cocktail lounge, Earline furtively and swiftly dropped to the rubber mat flooring behind the bar and ambled up the imitation pecan paneling which constituted the actual façade of the bar counter itself. Just as soon as she perceived no threat from any predator, she nestled under the very common denominator which we have all come to know and love, the tattered and very poorly-patched naugahyde elbow cushion located at the front of the bar.

On that very day, for the first time in her existence, with her eyes wide open, Earline had a chance to see and hear humans, her first such experience. She was somewhat stunned. Flabbergasted. In fact she was taken aback and perplexed as to how to enter this in her journal. She was not certain if she was living in the proper mode of life, living in *Naugahyde Hills*.

That evening, she penned in her diary that she had moved into a new home and with all of her eyes wide open, observed humans spending uncountable hours and dollars taking on immeasurable liquids, and saying nothing interesting. She also learned that they even have names, like we earwigs do. She thought that perhaps they were christened after great uncles like hers. Perhaps there is an Uncle Shithead, or maybe a great Uncle Asshole. (Those are two of the humans she saw and heard). *Humans are truly different. What funny names!*

A Bug on a Bar-Room Wall

Chapter Two
Cockroach Meets Earwig

"Roy"

There was moiling a sizeable and noisy gaggle of drunks on a Friday night in the third week of February. Darkness had fallen and the band had commenced doing what it always did, play loud music. The portly and pitiful bar proprietor must have been living on adrenalin. The wretch had been busy most of the day pouring watered-down bourbon into name-brand bottles, buying beer by the case at Costco and short sheeting the bank for the night bartender. It is amazing that he still had the temerity and stamina to roost by the entry door with his palm out, asking his regulars to pay a cover charge, to come in and support his business.

The big difference perceivable to Earline was that there was a layer of smoke in the lounge. She wondered why humans took smoke into their respiratory system. She knew of no other animals on Earth that did this. Neither birds, insects, nor mammals do this, at least not on purpose.

Earline started feeling the beat of the music. She began to sense an unusual tingling sensation of femininity from deep within her hyena. The strains and melodies masked her terror and discomfort of the diesel and supercharger. Rather, they stirred a tiny arousal in her complicated thigh system. She noticed that she had never quite felt like this in the past. She had, of course met and observed many other insects in her brief sojourn in Clairemont and in the walk-in-cooler but had not given much time or attention to any single one of them. Perhaps, she thought, I could use a friend.

The band droned on to the haunting lilt of an R&B slow number, like "Only You", by the Platters. Along sashayed a figure so imposing that she was stricken breathless. As he crawled from his security in a dirty bar towel hamper, he immediately caught her eyes with his confident swagger. She knew he was a different sort because of his walk, his number of legs, and his immense feelers. She noticed that he had more bridgework than the River Kwai. He seemed cocksure though a bit smug. He told her that his name was Roy, and his ancestors had lived in this bar for about twenty generations. She thought that he might be a fine addition to *Naugahyde Hills,* as he seemed to be the most magnificent figure she had ever seen. She wondered if he could possibly be the friend she so desperately needed and her heart fluttered as she eyed his differences and mannerisms. So big. So different. Beautiful!

He asked her if she would care to dance. She demurred. They wandered down the bar, antennae in antennae, to the perilous expanse of the parquet oak floor beneath the rotating glass ball of mirrors, dodging open-toed shoes as well as Wallabies. As the band began to waft enchanting tunes and riffs, she began to feel at ease and safe in the comfort of his many legs. He seemed so confident, yet tender, so gentle yet strong. She felt herself perched on the verge of a misty trance.

Roy asked her if she would like to go for a ride with him. At first she had trepidation, thinking back to the delivery truck, but relented. She wanted more from this new creature. She wanted excitement and adventure. She wanted company.

Earline loved the way Roy whispered into her brown little ear holes. Cockroaches possess exceedingly long thread-like antennae, oft-times longer than the hull of their bodies. These seem to be, in the male, geared for sexual recognition. They seemed to be working.

"Only you"

Saturday morning, early, as Roy and Earline shook cobwebs from their memories of the previous night their collective eyes were just sensing light. She flashed back to tender moments

A Bug on a Bar-Room Wall

from the dance floor. She recalled Roy whisking her off the floor and into the cuff of the pants of the bar owner. It was a wild ride, she remembered, and sighed. She peered from the vantage of the cuff in a double worsted pant leg, heaped in a pile at the foot of the bed of the bar owner. The cuff still had the delicious flavor of Ragu spaghetti sauce, which he had spilled on himself only a few days earlier. The owner would often make a hasty trot across the boulevard to eat Italian. When he was a child, his mother often fed him with a slingshot.

Earline became concerned that the two of them might not be able to find their way back to *Naugahyde Hills*. Roy assured her that she had no worries. He had devised a plan. He showed her how to conceal herself, between celery and romaine on a food platter destined for the bar that very afternoon. Roy let her know that if she had any problems, he would be amongst the pickles and radishes. They spent the next four hours frolicking in the tossed green salad and making memories as only lovers do. Roy muttered to her that he hoped last night was as good for her as it was for him. She did not know how to respond. She still had that warm and soupy feeling one gets, especially around all of her legs and her angina.

Someone had given the bar owner a "Where's Waldo?" game for his birthday and it seemed as if his head was going to explode from the hunt. His wife was sitting in a tub of lime Jello, trying shrink therapy. Their home routine on game day rarely varied. The owner and his wife prepared a buffet tray for a spread at the bar. The regulars always had to provide the meat and the labor. Today was birthday day for all of the regulars born in February, as well as the Pro-Bowl football game from

Honolulu. This was the time that the owner liked to audition loud rock bands. Of course he did this because the band played for free, and because it pissed off his regulars.

Earline remained somewhat puzzled about the meaning of their night together, and if perhaps it was loneliness or a real need. She had never felt quite like the way that Roy had made her feel, even though at two months of age, she was mature and able to ovulate. She wondered if this was what the humans meant when they used the term, *getting some.* She remembered thinking how silly this position was, not seeing his face and having his antennae wildly entangled in hers as he penetrated her hawse pipe with his gigantic annulary.

She noticed a few med flies hanging around their salad sanctuary. Her only previous sighting of med flies was around the floor safe in the office, where of course the owner stashed his cash and his kielbasa. It was there that Roy told her a little about his past, and some of his goals. He was from a long-established local family. Good roach stock. He was also a Navy veteran, like Uncle Earl, though not a Submariner. He had spent a tour on the mighty aircraft carrier Constellation, infesting cargo holds of potatoes from Idaho. His chief ambition was to organize the labor pool of roaches in this particular cocktail lounge.

As roaches go, she seemed to think that his leadership and charm made him fit for that job. At that moment, she reflected on whether or not her eggs had been fertilized, and in the ensuing two week gestation period would she deliver a Litter of *Cockwigs, or Earches?*

A Bug on a Bar-Room Wall

Of a sudden, the huge bowl of tossed green leafy vegetables with anchovies and liver was covered by a giant silver foil lid, and like Cain and Abel, the two of them, as well as a few med flies, were cast into the darkness. Into the sweltering trunk of a run-down Toyota went the bowl, rattling against a set of stolen Taylor-Made, golf clubs, surrounded by soiled sweat socks and empty plastic motor oil containers. This trip was not in a condominium, however, or worsted pants cuff. Earline felt great relief at the prospect of returning to her beloved *Naugahyde Hills*. Again she would behold the familiar sights of funnels and Kahlua bottles, some pissed-off regulars and again watching the owner turn the volume down until the patrons had to try to read the lips of John Madden and Pat Summerall. Owners. Are they not unique? When this one smokes, he blows onion rings!

At the festivities that day, Roy, Earline and some Med flies barely escaped being devoured by one of the patrons. This guy had recently retired from a well-known local lumber company and had little in the way of commodities in his home refrigerator, thus, was pretty active on the buffet circuit. Safely ensconced in *Naugahyde Hills* they bid each other goodnight, tenderly kissing through her fabric screen door. As she lay on her pillow, she had to listen to the ramblings of the owner conducting a dialogue with a painter. He told the painter what a squeaky-clean place he had here. The painting contractor replied that if it were any colder in here, you would have twice as many kinds of pests and vermin than you already have. Earline smiled.

Roy was in the twilight of slumber in the opinion page of the Union Tribune when he heard the immortal words denoting

Last Call. They were uttered of course at closing time. Earline finally nodded off under her elbow padding in *Naugahyde Hills*. She had truly found a new life away from the damp swabs at Mesa Distributing. In her dreams she made plans of contingency for the event of egg laying. She had earlier noticed warmth emanating from the satellite tuner, a perfect place to deliver a family of *Cockwigs*. Since the owner had no clue as to how to operate it, the family would be perfectly safe amongst the microchips and circuit boards. She slept.

"Willie"

A Bug on a Bar-Room Wall

Chapter Three
Bartenders, Strange Bedfellows

"Former bar owner Moe"

As her curiosity blossomed regarding humans, Earline wondered if the people who worked on one side of *Naugahyde Hills* were anything like the people who sat on the other side, all day. In the first week of March, a former owner of the *Naugahyde Hills* Cocktail lounge was expounding on how much he knew about bartenders. His expertise and limitless knowledge intrigued Earline so much that she tried to parse the words to describe him to mama in her journal The former owner was suffering several paper cuts on his tongue. His comments were acerbic. He drank vodka and lemon juice, provoking whimpers and cries of pain during his orations.

A Bug on a Bar-Room Wall

His name was Moe, and he was a long, tall, hulk of a man, who was so mean that most folks believed that he had been born with no anus. They felt that that was why he was so nasty all the time. There was no more room inside of his lanky frame because he was so full of himself. He had a reputation of having kindness to no other human being.

You would need a tetanus shot if you ever sipped from his jar. Moe opined that we go into bars to pass time in a pleasant atmosphere, to become anonymous, to chum with others on this ship of fools, or maybe to snuff out a lonely feeling we might have in other places. Earline got the idea that Moe was absolutely the smartest, most knowledgeable human she had ever heard expounding on bartenders, even smarter than Roy.

Moe droned on that the one common denominator in any joint, at any given time is the bartender on duty. He said that the duty bartender can set your mood for the rest of the day with just a few kind words, *or he can also stab you with an ice pick.* At that point, Earline noticed a little white spittle beginning to form around his lip corners. "It seems like when I enter a bar the person behind the bar usually greets me by my first name. He might say hey Moe, how have you been? Or he may substitute how was your day? (Unless I am at Lindbergh Field where they always call me Mac.) Maybe they all think my name is Mac. They are all named Pal. Every one of them!" He implied that he hated them all like sand in his eyes.

A Bug on a Bar-Room Wall

Earline began the preliminary steps of a double take, tightening up her short horny forewings, her pair of forceps at the terminal end of her abdomen, and even her biting mouthparts. She wondered where Moe was coming from. Furthermore, Moe recounted his view that nurses, doctors, teachers, contractors and the like are considered professionals and would add to this list, lawyers, painters, tap cleaners, boil suckers, manicurists, insulators and single fathers. Moe seemed to have a lot of opinions. He thought that crude oil was a pollutant. He thought Arabs should run the world. He thought bars should never subscribe to a newspaper because then the bartenders might know what is on TV. Moe thought all women had but one function. He thought the state owed everyone everything. His chief belief was that he was the smartest, handsomest man in history.

It appeared abundantly clear to Earline that Moe had plenty of opinions. He added to the list of helping professionals, the professional bartender. It was clearly a fact to him that if a person does not truly love dealing with people of all kinds they should not be considered a helping professional. One of his eyes rolled to the back of his septic head. He wondered if one could imagine a San Diego County Sheriff hating people in general? So it is behind the bar. So it is throughout the world. (Except maybe in this joint.)

At this point, Earline began to wonder if she was in the right lounge, or if *Naugahyde Hills* was truly the place where she belonged. Moe figured that many bartenders seem dead from the neck up but their input is still critical. This is at times such as when it comes time to relay a funny story, help answer a

A Bug on a Bar-Room Wall

trivia question, spread filthy gossip about who is doing who, or just plain make things up. Bartenders are not gender limited. A real bartender is essentially sexless. (Especially here.) No matter that a bartender is a man or a woman, these little services are the main ingredients for this Ciopino.

The nodding of his head got a little more violent as he started believing what he was saying. He continued that it was little things like wiping the neck of a beer bottle with a napkin before setting it in front of a customer. Moe had often wondered what they were wiping off. Maybe roach droppings?

At this, Earline did all she could to maintain her composure, and broke a nail trying to speed-write into her diary. She conjured up images of her beloved Roy leaving droppings on bottlenecks. Disgusting, she thought. Moe continued that just knowing what to put into a glass or opening a jar of beer did not require a doctorate. Quite frequently you will hear of a bartender with a following or a reputation. Groupies. Homeboys. Sycophants all. There is a lady tending bar over on Jackson Drive in La Mesa who is reputed to make the best bloody Mary in the world. It is not universally understood where she got this alleged reputation. Maybe she just made it up and says so.

There is a concrete cutter working in a bar up on Lake Murray Boulevard who tends bar skunk-faced, plays the juke box at twelve decibels above the threshold of pain and serves up a crock pot of food every bit as good as that served over at "Doo Daas" in Encanto.

A Bug on a Bar-Room Wall

There is another over on University at Harbison, which has hired two of the hottest babes in the State of California. Their Margaritas are lethal. Good enough to give you a bladder infection. Moe droned on. Earline felt sickened. Moe related that the daygirl there does not care much for him any more. She stuck a dinner fork in the back of his left hand and pushed a plate of hot yams over into the crotch of his double knit pants. He reiterated that he does not think she likes him.

By this time, there were a few patrons who had assembled at the feet of Moe, so to speak. Earline noticed that the group included painters, laggers, home inspectors, and other criminals. Earline wished that her Roy could be there to hear all of this. She also remembered his soft, flat-bodied torso and his magnificent sensitive feelers.

A great, white skinned human, chock full of hubris, with a booming voice and crystal clear hair chimed in that he knew of a place in Sisters, Oregon where the night bartender was electrocuted when a ground wire came loose in her vibrator. Her sister worked over in Lake Shasta, from the same accident-prone family. She was working as a beer-cart driver in a bar golf tournament and was run over by the same cart nine times. She seemed to be having a run of bad luck. Earline had a tough time trying to understand all of these turns of events with regard to bartenders. She started to think that maybe they were even stranger than owners, or customers, if that were possible. The only specie stranger, that she had first hand witnessed, was the former owner. Roy agreed.

Moe finally went home and left a mouth-breathing group sitting at the bar. Even more expert witnesses wandered in, waiting their alternate turns at describing bartenders. Another lagger piped in that he had been in a bar the other day over on Garnett in Pacific Beach and noticed that there were two bartenders on the same shift. It was not due to the heavy business volume, it was because the owner had hired a set of Siamese twins, connected at the forehead. While nobody has seen their faces they maintain a constant dialogue with each other.

The lady that operates the bar over on Baltimore Drive puts out terrific S.O.S. on Saturdays. On Sundays she just puts out. The home inspector walked in and announced that he had just finished a job in the Mission Bay area and had stopped for a beer. The bar was called *Chappaquidicks* and is only a few backstrokes from the Coast Guard pier. He felt that a place like that ought to have a large selection of registered nurses, lonely wives, confused runaways, and of course plenty of itinerant painters and thirsty insulators. The home inspector, of course, noticed Earline peeping her little jowls out of the Naugahyde. He was just too nice to disrupt the balance of nature. (Especially in this dump, where it was so fragile already that a loud fart would cause chaos.)

This owner was so cheap that at Christmastime he would save on tinsel. Instead, he would prop Moe up near the tree and encourage him to sneeze. This would elicit whoops of delight from the many bail bondsmen who frequented the bar.

A Bug on a Bar-Room Wall

"Owner of worsted Bib overalls"

A Bug on a Bar-Room Wall

Chapter Four
Jack Mac has Baggage

Out in East San Diego County, at a seedy little cocktail lounge on Wintergardens Boulevard, a huge Peterbilt fifth wheeler pulled in for the regularly scheduled Monday delivery. It was about ten in the morning. Frank, the Teamster knew he had a rough day ahead. His load of barrels and cases of beer made for a physical strain, off-loading the kegs and boxes and delivering them to their appropriate destinations. (Never the same from bar to bar).

Secreted in the cargo, hiding in a case of Corona Beer from Mexico were a pair of innocent stow-aways; Melvin Smith, the oldest brother of Earline, as well as their sister, Kathy. They too, would soon experience the feeling of weightlessness, as Frank would heft the Corona cases to his dolly. Nervousness abounded as they were hustled through the rutted parking lot, over the pitted threshold, around the tattered pool tables, past the groaning juke box and alongside the rancid popcorn maker and crammed into a tiny, dark storage closet containing more cases of beer, kegs, CO_2 bottles, hoses and miscellaneous lost and found items. These included jackets, hats, sweaters, pool-stick satchels, eyeglasses, dead cell phones and a few threadbare purses. The only humans to ever enter this space were the deliveryman, the morning swamper who stocked the bar, and an occasional bartender who infrequently had to service the taps.

As Frank stood at the end of the bar, trying to collect the cash for his shipment order, he made small talk with one of the decrepit regulars, Jack Mac. They briefly discussed the Lakers, the Padres, the Chargers, the War, Women, Finance, Law, Chemistry, and Religion. After one minute and forty seconds their combined inventory of knowledge had been expended. They bid each other *adieu*.

"Jack Mac"

A Bug on a Bar-Room Wall

Jack Mac was in the autumn of his years, approaching ninety-six years of age. His routine of habituating this lounge was becoming a tedious and arduous daily chore, considering all of the liver damage he was sustaining with the copious consumption of Absolut vodka. Jack would often hustle drinks on the pool table and was considered an excellent shot-maker, combining a keen eye and many years of practice. His was a feather soft, accurate shot. He would talk to the ladies in a grandfatherly manner and on occasion would even glide them around the dance floor. Unlike Fernando, who danced like a frightened Kangaroo, Jack was smooth, even slick. Jack had forgotten what he had done for a living but it was of no consequence since he never seemed to spend any money.

As he commiserated with his fellow parishioner, Willie, the earth was shaken by the ear-splitting noise of a beer-keg going dry. The blast was so piercing and shrill that it nearly petrified the two stow-aways, Melvin and Kathy. They instantly scurried from their relatively secure hiding place in the Corona box to an even more snug refuge, the pool stick case belonging to Jack Mac himself.

Jack Mac had long been planning to relocate himself and his meager belongings to the East, wanting to spend his final retirement with his early life-chums and relatives, drinking his Absolut in clubs, holding fond memories of his younger days working for the railroad, and enjoying the seasons.

The following are some excerpts from the diary he kept upon his relocation:

A Bug on a Bar-Room Wall

Dear Diary

August 12: Got out of the bar business for good. Do not have to deal with turds like Willie, Ben, Mitch or those other clowns. It is so beautiful here! The mountains are majestic. I can hardly wait to see winter come, along with the snow! I will never miss those Santa Ana winds of Southern California.

October 14: This has got to be the most beautiful place since Eden! The trees are all of the shades of red and orange. Saw some deer romping this morning. What graceful and elegant creatures. This must be Heaven. I love it so! There are no real deer in San Diego.

November 11: Deer season opens tomorrow. I cannot imagine killing such gorgeous animals, Hope it snows soon. Why would someone shoot a deer?

December 2: Last night it snowed! Everything was blanketed with white, like in a Christmas card from the NRA. I went out and cleaned the snow off of the stairs and shoveled the driveway. What a beautiful place, Hornell, New York! A snowplow came by and blew snow to the sides. Had to shovel the driveway again.

December 12: More snow last night. I love it! The snowplow did his thing to the driveway again.

December 19: Covered with snow again last night. Could not get out of the driveway to go to the American Legion. 1 am exhausted from shoveling the driveway. Damned snowplow!

A Bug on a Bar-Room Wall

The Legion seems to be crawling with earwigs anyway.

December 22: More of that white shit fell last night. I have blisters on my hands from operating that shovel. I think the snowplow hides around the corner till I am through shoveling my driveway. Asshole! I wish I were back in Lakeside.

"Jack Mac in Hornell, N.Y."

A Bug on a Bar-Room Wall

December 25: Merry fucking Christmas! Eight more inches of that Goddamn snow! If I ever get my hands on that son-of-a-bitch that drives that snowplow, I swear I will kill that bastard! Do not know why they do not use more salt on the roads to melt the treacherous fucking ice!

December 27: Been inside for two full days, except while shoveling off the driveway every time that Goddamn plow passes by. Cannot go anywhere, including that bug-infested American Legion to get a drink! Wonder where all the fucking earwigs came from? My car is submerged under a pile of that white shit! Weatherman says to expect ten more inches tonight. Asshole! I would rather deal with Concrete Pete than put up with this stuff!

December 28: The weatherman was wrong. 34 inches! This shit will not melt until the fourth of July! Christ! The snowplow got stuck on a curb and the prick came to my door to borrow a shovel. After I told him I had broken four shovels while clearing out the shit he left in my driveway I broke my last one across his neck.

January 4: Finally got out of the house today. Went to the club to get a drink. An exterminator truck was parked at the club spraying for earwigs. On the way home I had a collision with an eight-point buck. Did about $3,000.00 damage to the front of my car. Fucking beasts! They should all be shot and killed! Goddamn I miss my club in San Diego. Willie was right.

May 3: Took the car to the garage in Hornell. Would you believe the Goddamn thing is rusted out from all of the

A Bug on a Bar-Room Wall

Goddamn salt those idiots spread all over the roads? Where am I?

May 10: Moving back to Lakeside. Cannot imagine anyone in his or her right mind wanting to live in the fucking State of New York! I plan to die sitting on a bar stool alongside Willie McGee.

Chapter Five
Earline & Tank

The dart team started assembling their group around seven in the evening. It was composed of three women and three men. All of them were Lounge Lizards. They had driven the short distance from their home bar over on El Cajon Boulevard. This place was on one of the corners where streetwalkers were often photographed with their Johns, and had their mugs published in the local gazette. This was a new tactic by the La Mesa Police to curb prostitution. Since Earline had heard many various descriptions of different bars, she felt a yen to somehow visit another bar for further confirmation; but how, by what manner of conveyance?

Earline decided to let Roy know of her thoughts. She figured that he might have a useful suggestion with his vast experience in these matters. After all, she was trying to document her experiences for Mama Dina. Roy seemed to be worried, but quite understanding. How are you going to get there and back? She replied that she had no clue, but thought maybe he could conjure up a plan. He asked her what she was trying to confirm. Earline thought long and hard, and told him that she wanted to see with her own eyes if other owners are as inane as this one, if bartenders elsewhere are as goofy as the crew in this one, and if patrons were all similar and finally, if other places are as run down and tawdry as this crater. Here, she intoned, they have a sign on the wall that tells people not to spit on the floor, it leaks. Roy told her he would give it some thought.

At first, Roy was quite disconcerted at the thought of being separated from his newly found love, though she had rebounded well after their first foray in the worsted cuff. He feared losing her to another roach, or even another earwig. He felt jealousy. He felt vibrations that he was not accustomed to. He thought and thought. He felt like he was being tested. He took a long walk under the Naugahyde and ran some schemes through his clever mind. He rejected many notions as too risky, too dangerous, too silly, or too selfish. Finally, he returned to her in her satellite tuner and told her he had a plan.

Roy told Earline that he had an excellent view of the bar and had her join him to take in the vista. He pointed his muscular pointer at the dartboard, where there was some action. He told her that the shaggy fellow in the plaid shirt would be her ticket to ride. He was talking about the guy with the scrubby beard and the shaggy russet colored hair. His name was Tank and he was approaching the board to retrieve his darts. Roy pointed him out to Earline and told her that Tank was a member of the visiting team, and would be likely to return for a rematch later in the season. That means that if you can hitch a ride in his Fruit of the Looms, you would be able to get from here to there and back again with no apparent problems. Earline sighed at the simplicity of this plan and at the clever way that Roy seemed to handle challenges. Roy figured that if all went well, he would see her again within about a week with her logs, journals and impressions of the other world, the world of Jim Stewart.

Earline surveyed the man carefully. She observed his pockmarked face and was reminded of the surface of the moon. His shock of dirty hair lacked the luster of the mop, in which took life. He had a wobbly way of letting go of his darts, often lodging them in the gypsum board adjacent to the target. He had a quiet demeanor and somehow seemed different from the other humans. He was not an adroit darts man, somewhat shaky. She eyed him cautiously acknowledging that she would be putting her life in his hands. She overheard one of his teammates refer to him as Tank. She thought about the name. "Could there be a great uncle Tank?"

"Tank"

The evening ticked on. Tank downed a few pure tequilas and of course helped his team to lose the match. The upside of this was that in his numbness he did not notice Earline shinny up his sleeve, down his Pendleton collar and into the dark dungeons of his underwear, there to nestle in his Fruit of the Loom crotch pouch, in the warmth and darkness of his cod sack, to await her next adventure.

A Bug on a Bar-Room Wall

It seemed warm and musky down there against his tumescent yet throbbing system. She could feel and hear his heart pumping. His pulse rate seemed to rise and fall with the approach of each of his turns at the dartboard. She could also feel his warm and throbbing system increase rates as he followed the woman in front of him. She was a very pleasant woman who had an equally soft touch with her dart throwing hand. She always appeared to be smiling and was quick to let everyone know that they were all welcome in her bar. She must have been another owner. Tank was in a state of confusion, probably induced by the Jose Cuervo. He was not worried so much about losing the match. He was a little more concerned about losing his job. He was an itinerant tap cleaner who could not foresee the next five-dollar bill to cross his palm.

As most of us possibly know, the common cockroach is in the order of Orthoptera, and has narrow and thickened wings, folded sideways, though they rarely fly. Roy could not fly anyway, because he had been grounded in the reserves. Their metamorphosis is quite simple and their mouthparts are not sucking or vestigial, but chewing. This endeared the memory to Earline as he was considered big in the size department, and the earwig was always described as small to medium. She was from the Dermaptera order. Her wings were also short, thick and folded. (Earline smiled faintly as she recalled their differences). She nodded off to sleep in the pima cotton underwear, feeling as if this might be an evening she would not soon forget. The last thing she remembers hearing was someone declaring Last Call.

A Bug on a Bar-Room Wall

Chapter Six
Tank Tanks

"Tanking"

Around two AM the adventures of Earline and Tank truly began. Tank was maneuvering his Bronco from the visited bar to his miserable home. He lit a Camel, inched his way out of his parking place, turned on the headlights, turned on some country music and while reaching across to roll down the window, drove directly into the driver's side door of a parked La Mesa Police Department cruiser, which was parked in front of a Baker's Square Restaurant.

Rather than a short ride in a Bronco, in some underwear, Earline was treated to a field sobriety test, replete with the toe to heel, the ten paces out and back, and the alphabet dilemma. Tank did not excel in any of these events. Earline got her next ride in the rear seat of a black and white Ford Galaxie. It had the smell of disinfectant, like a cheap peep show. There was no conversation. Upon arrival at the San Diego County Jail, Tank was booked, fingerprinted, strip-searched and led to a dry-out cell for a nap. She had clung to her precious hiding place with all of her might until he again donned his shorts and his jail issued coveralls. He was given a blood test for his sobriety screening and restlessly slept. She bit tightly with her tiny teeth to avoid being shaken out of her secret hiding place, never noticing the moisture in the very garment she was clinging to.

Now, she thought she would have to stay with this man for whatever duration or she would be forever lost in here. Once relocated to a holding cell he slept fitfully. He tossed and turned on his steel seat bench, always keeping one eye open, watching for predators or thieves. Little did Tank know that there was more to come from his voluntary blood test than a blood alcohol ratio. There was a small matter of testing HIV Positive!

Earline wondered if she too, could be HIV Positive. Insects of many types are generally immune to most human afflictions, and are even resistant to radiation. She had ingested body fluids from his Fruit of the Looms and made a mental note to ask Roy about it if she ever saw him again. She got no further rides until about noon on the second day. He was released and got a Yellow Cab ride to Hillcrest. It was here that she sneaked out of his shorts and into the shaggy mane of hair behind his starboard ear. The very first thing Tank did upon egress from the Yellow Cab was pay the man and enter the bar on University at Richmond. He ordered and inhaled a Ceurvo Gold get well shot. He sighed. She sighed.

A Bug on a Bar-Room Wall

Tank then called a friend from the opposing dart team and arranged for a ride to rescue his impounded Bronco. It was barely damaged, but cost him nearly his last dollar to rescue it. Astonishingly, he then proceeded to the scene of the crime and went in for one more shot. Earline could not believe her feelers! She was home! She waited for an opportune time when he was looking at the TV set with a game show blaring, the owner gawking and the bartender eating a pickled egg. She jumped ship, and slid under the safety of *Naugahyde Hills.*

There had been two strikes on the wretched Tank at the very time he failed to show up for work. In fact, he knew that he was doomed as soon as he felt the handcuffs. He realized that he could not keep his pitiful little job cleaning beer systems with no driver's license. Tank was fired at two PM that afternoon and given his last paycheck. More Cuervo Gold.

Just like a mouse in your pocket or a fly on the wall, *or an earwig under your elbow rest,* Earline sensed that there would be more problems. She had missed Roy. She had even missed her flatulent owner. She felt remorse for her adventure, but still enjoyed the excitement. Tank, on the other hand sort of felt that the end was at hand. He had not mentioned the HIV virus to any of his pals. Most of them had noticed his physical appearance and simply wrote it off to tequila consumption without much food intake. Little did they know, the sinister nature of this problem that Tank dealt with was about to drive him to the edge. He had been a pretty good tap-cleaner though it was not the steadiest of trades. He knew his tools and required very little supervision. This was to be his worst day. He had, of course reached high points in his life, earlier, when he felt useful and handsome. He had been deeply in love and even made a baby, though he failed to raise it. Lately he had been feeling that he flailed away at most of his challenges and could not seem to come away with a victorious feeling.

For some reason, unexplainable, Earline reflected upon all of her recent excitement. It was no where near mundane, and realized that she thrived on it. It gave her female sacristy a warm and mellow feeling. She slipped back out from under *Naugahyde Hills,* up the Pendleton sleeve and clung to a hank of dirty hair in his armpit. She discovered that she truly craved adventure!

When Tank drank heavily he seemed to become a completely different man. He would pass from Jekyll to Hyde in a short time span. He could barely read a scrabble tile without moving his lips. Like most men, he thought he was a great guy, but if truth be told, that was only in his mind. On this day, as he swilled tequila, a few memories emerged in his mind like the remains of a wreck at low tide.

Tank did not have a perfect life. His only son from two marriages was not known to him as a child. He knew him as a little leaguer or a Pop Warner player, but never in his formative years. It looked as though Tank was about to become the pyre of any excitement Earline could be seeking.

The man was tired, disappointed with his cruel fate and dreading all of the ramifications involved with his latest DUI. He was quite loveless, with nobody to intimately squeeze. His organ had not been working as designed, lately. This is how, in his fifties, he found himself sitting in his Bronco, with the motor running, in his garage, with the vacuum cleaner hose venting exhaust gasses through his wing window. This was how Tank ended his misery. Hoisted on his own petard with an earwig sitting on his ear.

A Bug on a Bar-Room Wall

Chapter Seven
A Reprieve

Earline instantly deduced that she had hitched her wagon to the wrong star. There she was, poised, on the dusty dashboard of a well-worn Ford Bronco. She noticed a mild rash on her centrifugal and immediately decided to escape by fleeing the scene. (She apparently made many rash judgments.) The poor waif hurried down the great catenary of vacuum hose, much like weary wharf rats abandon a troubled vessel. She had trepidation about her well-being and futurity and knew nothing about her environment or her next possible action. Her only consideration, immediately, was to be rid of the awful scene of mortality lost.

Though a mere couple of hours had passed, she lurked behind a 75R-15 Goodyear steel belted radial snow tire and anxiously awaited the next adventure. Earline finally discerned the mournful wail of a distant siren. It seemed to be coming from the nearby Interstate corridor. Events transpired rather quickly. First to arrive, of course was the black and white belonging to the La Mesa Police Department, who immediately put out a few calls. Subsequent to his arrival, came the tall, slender representative from the offices of the County Coroner. He knew his job, and exactly what to do next. The Coroner was dressed in tan Dockers, with a polo shirt, windbreaker and a TwinPac baseball cap. He drove a maroon Ford Explorer. He was eating Pistachio nuts. The two men bagged Tank, in all of his glory and placed his carcass in the SUV for further disposition. Tank had reached ambient temperature and took his final ride in a maroon Ford Explorer.

A Bug on a Bar-Room Wall

With the Explorer gone, and the Bronco going nowhere, Earline was faced with another command decision. She quickly eyed the black and white Ford Galaxy, sized-up the ruddy complexioned, stocky driver and commenced the make-up-your-mind process that females often do. He was wearing travatan colored twill trousers, complete with hot sauce stains from the Alberto Gold Star Burrito Stand #17, over on Lake Murray Boulevard. This member of the La Mesa Police Department looked and smelled familiar to her. Could he be one and the same man who had cuffed (in more ways than one) Tank, only two days earlier? Her heart quickened. She could scarcely believe the coincidence.

Could it be that off duty police officers frequented bars? Might he be her Ark of Noah for a return to *Naugahyde Hills?* Could it possibly be that she had learned her lesson, and would be able to stifle her craving for excitement? Could she book passage for a return to her beloved roach? She felt pangs in her autoclave and actually longed to be safely in his clutches. With rapid thinking and some adroit maneuvers, she slipped from her vantage behind the rear snow tire, through a shadow and up his Frye Boot. She made a frantic leap across to the threadbare top of his argyle sock, and into the scrubby little hairs on his Tibia Major. Earline scaled his bony shinbone as if rock-climbing and deposited herself in an empty mace holder on his belt.

It was there she would stay, for the rest of his watch. He spent the next several hours doing the things police officers do while on duty; things such as eating, parking, watching things and making people nervous. Sometimes he practiced turning on his siren or speaker system. Sometimes he flirted with day bartenders under the cover of authority. On a few occasions he would look out the window to see if there were any high-speed chases going on. He was rarely that lucky. His day was actually quite boring, and except for the hassles he gave to temporary parkers, he had little fun on his shifts. Today he decided to strike and spread fourteen road flares in a row up on University Avenue, and act as if there had been some sort of accident. (There was no accident). Then he would spend the next twenty minutes snuffing them out with his Frye Boot, as bewildered, nervous motorists cruised by, wondering what they had missed.

It was nearly 1600 hours PM as he prepared to turn in his clipboard at the station, change out of his togs, and dash for Miller Time, to boast about his nefarious exploits of the day. Other than his ordinary and routine habitual haunts, he chose this day to drop in on *Naugahyde Hills,* to see if he could possibly inject into a conversation that he had arrested one of their customers for running into his police cruiser and strangely enough discovered the poor devil dead two days later. It seemed sure to make Officer Tooty the star of the show. It did.

Chapter Eight
Master Sergeant Murray -USMC

Bob Silvo, a crack salesman for Mesa Distributing had half a dozen calls on his Monday agenda. North County was one of the choice territories for any liquor salesman. It contained the cities of Escondido, San Marcos, Fallbrook, Carlsbad and Vista, The plum of this account was in none of these cities. The plum of this account was the US Marine Corps base at Camp Joseph Pendleton, in Oceanside, California. These people consumed more beer and alcohol than the entire Navy contingent in the county, including the Submarine Base!

Bob had at least one simple call to make that day taking orders for delivery on Friday. His calls included the Enlisted Men's Club, The NCO Club, The Master Sergeant's Club, The Junior Officer's Club, The Officer's Club, The Flag Officer's Club, The Chaplain's Club, The Officer's Wife's Club, The Enlisted Men's Wives Club and of course the Civil Servant's Club.

While calling on the Master Sergeant's Club, he asked for some help unloading a very special premium for the bar. The Sergeant in charge assigned two privates to help retrieve it from Bob's Company SUV. They uncrated it, as directed, in the pool hall. It drew all of the attention of the management as well as the customers. The premium, once unwrapped, was a replica of the hood of Dale Earnhart's Budweiser NASCAR rig. It was designed to be a light system over one of their many pool tables. The entire place erupted in applause, and Bob Silvo was indeed the man of the hour! Maybe even the hero of Pendleton that day. Dozens of marines of all ages clamored to have a peek at the treasure. Excelsior and Styrofoam littered the adjacent dance floor as well as 1" by 4" broken pine, crating material.

All eyes were focused on the gleaming red colors, the Budweiser logo, and the number 8! Hoots and Ooyas went up, as if the war had ended. Not one of the sharp-eyed Marines, not even the snipers, spotted the two little specks on the dance floor, running for their lives to the nearest carpet coverage. They found sanctuary in the starched fatigue belt line of Master Sergeant Jack Murray. Murray was, of course perched atop a stool nearest the exit. This was his habit. It had been his habit since Korea, Viet Nam and his first tour with the Thundering Herd in Iraq. From his ample belt line, the two little specks (earwigs Cathy and Matthew), there was a mad dash to take cover in Master Sergeant Murray's shorts.

All hands gleefully celebrated the remainder of the day. Rounds of drinks, three-ball tournaments, sea stories, more rounds of drinks and by 1500 PM, there was nobody fit to drive a vehicle except Bob Silvo and perhaps the two unnoticed earwigs. Bob went on to his appointed rounds and reported to his sales manager at Mesa, that afternoon that he had one of his biggest orders for Budweiser since he started working there.

Master Sergeant Murray hailed a base cab around 1600PM to get back to his off-base apartment in Oceanside. He knew that he had to stow his gear, as he was shipping out for his second tour in Iraq, and from his briefings, there was a major ass-kicking event coming up. He wanted to store up all of the sleep he could get. Murray took a short nap, showered, sobered up and turned in around 2100 PM. He had no live-in, as most Master Sergeants were wont to do. He had been on his own for what seemed like an eternity. From Chosin to Okinawa, from Hue City to Olongapo, from Camp Lejune to Kuwait, he had always been a loner. Sure, he liked to have a female around, on occasion, but he was married to the Corps and was the mother to his platoon. Besides, females were not government issued.

Matthew & Cathy did not want to interfere with the Master Sergeant or become conspicuous in any way. They had no clue about their imminent travels and proceeded to move into an olive drab, canvas sea bag, which looked like the snuggest, warmest quarters in the entire tiny apartment. Little did they know, they were about to embark on the trip of a lifetime. The next motion they sensed was as they were jostled, along with other fellow travelers into a waiting truck, with 180 other sea bags for delivery to buses where they and the others boarded for the winding drive through the California hills to March Air Force Base for the trip East.

These men were one of the most storied units in the Corps: 3rd Battalion, 1st Marine Regiment, nicknamed The Thundering Herd. This was truly the next Greatest Generation, as Tom Brokaw had put it. Five months after being deployed to Iraq, Lima Company's 1st platoon found itself in Fallujah, with Master Sergeant Murray and two earwigs in heavy action. They were embroiled in some of the most intense house-to-house combat since World War II. Civilians were used as human shields or as bait to lure soldiers into buildings rigged with explosives; Suicide bombers approached from every corner hoping to die and take Americans with them; Radical insurgents, high on adrenaline and narcotics, fought to the death. Murray's platoon and his earwigs were among the first to fight in Fallujah, and they bore the brunt of this epic battle. When it was over, the platoon had suffered thirty-five casualties, including four dead.

During one of their episodes, Master Sergeant Murray had spotted scores of Mujahideen pouring out of a large mosque from his rooftop vantage point. His two earwigs clung to his web belt, (it was unbearably hot in his skivvies). The muj were about to envelop the 3rd Platoon. They had run into a hornet's nest. About an hour before the ambush, one of Murray's men had discovered a children's ice cream truck loaded with a massive arsenal of weapons. They learned that it was not ice cream aboard; there were thirty RPGs, brand new Dragunov sniper rifles, mines, grenades and ammunition. The Trojan Horse and the vast majority of the Jihadists escorting it were suddenly vaporized by one well-placed Hellfire missile, called in by Master Sergeant Murray, Cathy and Matthew. It was time for a little rest.

Chapter Nine
They Did It

It was a cool murky winter evening in East San Diego, around 1800 PM. A ruddy faced, stocky man strolled into *Naugahyde Hills* for his getting off drink. He had, for several years, practiced this routine, habituating this spot on his way home from tiresome days of peculiar happenings. La Mesa's finest are of course constantly stressed. There are pressures foisted upon them by their superiors and the citizenry of La Mesa. Beside the morning suicide, he had just that morning helped a little blue haired dowager across Baltimore Drive (against her will) and fielded countless calls from irate La Mesans; it seemed to him that everyone was pissed off.

A machinist for example had called and wanted someone to help find his mountain bike, though it had but one wheel and many missing spokes. There was a convenience store owner who complained about someone who had pilfered a six-day-old Pastrami sandwich. A retired electrician moaned that his circuit breakers were incessantly tripping, and a Caltrans computer whiz whined that he was in big trouble because he could not get a bag of M&Ms open. Another man from Hillcrest moaned that he had been rear-ended the day before. Stress, big time.

As he noisily dragged out a stool at the hook of the bar, he quickly scanned his surroundings, as all police officers are trained to do. He wanted to know some details before he entered communications with anyone. To his left was seated an itinerant one-eyed handyman with a finger in one nostril. One seat further down, a comely brunette was chortling with a friend named Molly. To his immediate right sat a home inspector. He was not chortling with anyone, he was staring down the blouse of the weary bartendress complimenting her on her socks. La Mesas Finest rued his seat selection the instant his eyes adapted to the 40-watt lighting. Just as he was served his Budweiser, he espied some sort of insect scurrying beneath his elbows into the safe confines of the Naugahyde elbow rest. (Earline was home, for good).

Roy, her beloved roach, had no idea that his beloved Earline the earwig had returned from her journey not once, but twice! Roy normally hid in the substrata, not moving a leg or a feeler for days at a time. There was nothing busy about this bug. In fact he was as lazy as an Alaskan fisherman. He was constantly in hiding, avoiding daylight whenever he spotted the extermination people. (Which was a rare event in this joint). The cockroach is the bane of lounge operators throughout the world, because they imply filthy conditions. Most customers

A Bug on a Bar-Room Wall

however cackle with glee upon sight of one of the little creatures.

It was of little wonder, then, that a disturbance in his flux field instantly warned him of a penetration of his defensive perimeter. Roy could scarcely believe his feelers! Earline crept up amongst his massive legs and began sobbing uncontrollably. He assuaged her feelings. She slept. When her eyes fluttered open, she surveyed him with a mystic awe, an almost reverent aura. Earline derived some strange pleasure, knowing that just centimeters above where they lay sat many knobby, callused and flaky elbows. Her abdomen and her bitumenum felt aglow with an eerie delight. She just had to feel those thrills that accompany peril. She realized that she was a thrill seeker. Earline slid back into a foggy daydream. She imagined that just before twilight, from under the cushion, insects came out to stroll, feeler in feeler. She could hear the squeals of children playing, little cockwigs. She heard Willie Nelson wailing in the background. In the quieter corners, other lovers were sitting, touching one another's atriums. The hectic pace had slowed to a crawl. She finally felt at peace. She savored the moment and decided to do her nails. (All eighteen of them). Her wake up call would come soon enough. Again she slept.

The town drunks began arriving, some by twos, mostly alone. Roy could hear the cacophony in their home. The sounds were channeled through the convergence zones of the foam rubber padding. There were muted voices, clinking of glasses, clanking of cans and occasional guffaws. The evening air was full of cigarette smoke and thick with slurred speech. A few shouts, pool balls clicking, inane laughter, darts whizzing and

A Bug on a Bar-Room Wall

obscenities now and again interrupted Roy's tender endearments.

Roy's feelers swayed left right, left right until Earline filled all of his hairy fists. He then reached tenderly around her to take her rhododendron in his fingertips. He lightly stroked her canvas-like underbelly and elicited a few squeals of ecstasy. She was bending and arching under his weight and the weight of her recent ordeals. Her eyes rolled back in her head before her beautiful lashes slammed shut. She was glad that this tall, slightly graying specimen was about to insert his glaucoma into her brevity. He had a wonderful smile, almost a smug grin, though his personality more than made up for any potential defects that she might later perceive. His masculine body was so different than hers; it brought excitement to her pendulum. She dripped slightly. She felt faint. After everything she had seen in her apparition, she wanted to believe. She also deduced that she had felt a sense of excitement, and figured that he might satisfy her thirst for adventure. Her Roy.

As Earline remained in this trance- like state, she opined that Roy was of high birth, learned, had good knowledge in general, seemed successful, had formed closely guarded opinions and on occasion did the proper thing at proper times. He was a good storyteller, funny, witty, and quite eloquent. Roy was full of perseverance and usually free of any kind of anger. Roy seemed conservative and kind to children. He loved all sorts of sports and was apparently disease free. She wondered what sort of woman would not love to have a man like that. From her reverie, Earline felt that she had to learn if he was for real, or too good to be true.

A Bug on a Bar-Room Wall

Roy was about to wake her. He had never quite felt so sappy. He thought of Earline as a multi-legged Ann Margaret, just beautiful. He loved her voluptuous mandibles, her sinewy thighs, her vivacious plutonic, and most of all her apparent loyalty. It meant a lot to him. She was totally unlike the roaches he had visited with in the past. She was great fun to hang with and seemingly had no real temper. She was thoughtful and he adored her body segments. She had a fondness for the good qualities in other insects as well as a love of privacy and discretion. She was making him thermal in places he had never been warm before. He wondered if she was for real, or was she too good to be true?

He reached around and woke her by caressing her thymus. They did it.

Chapter Ten
A Pair to Draw To

Earline knew, naturally what was happening to her. She supposed that it was enjoyable, but there seemed to be a slight trace of disappointment in her mind. Roy had been quite clumsy and hurried in his delivery. His first experience with crossbreeding had not gone well. It appeared that though there had been some ecstasy, there had also been some trepidation.

He was clumsy and slightly crude. He did not appreciate the gentleness that earwigs require nor did he show much consideration for her feelings. He was, in a word, immature. She sobbed. Her hopes for a perfect mate were obviously dashed. She felt deeply that she had made a mistake.

Above them, the prattle and chatter droned on. The owner's wife said, "Stop picking that scab, Louie, or it will never heal!" "What the hell?" Louie replied, "It's *your* lip." The soufflé-haired owner needed a drug test and maybe a course in anger management. His missus had been so dour and ill tempered that he spent the majority of his honeymoon in a Lazy Boy recliner. She constantly accused him of boinking the bartenders or even other women, as if he could.

In the foam padding of *Naugahyde Hills,* Roy and Earline lay together in a layer of pinguid fluids. His cigar smelled up the scene unpleasantly. Earline wondered, is that all there is? She noticed that some of his tenderness had evaporated and given way to a near-smug mode. Had she done something wrong? He was enigmatic. He had been jovial but juvenile. He pointed out that he was her only friend. His stock did not rise. Her confidence was visibly shaken.

Above them, a retired truck driver asked a brown-haired lady if there was something new about her eyes. Mascara, replied the insurance lady. At precisely that moment, the insurance lady noticed a roach saunter across the bar and scurry down the plywood paneling which constituted the inner bar skin itself. Roy was off to gloat and glow. He felt as if he had done something useful. He had not.

As most folks are aware, the average life span of a cockroach spanned approximately sixty weeks. As Roy reached his forties, the sexual vitality that he once took for granted began to wane. He just had less interest in sex. Roy found himself spending less and less time with roachettes. His ability to achieve and maintain a resurrection declined with each week. His simple capacity to entwine feelers was nowhere near what it once was.

Roy was not into the popular drugs of the day, drugs for maintenance of ever-important erections. He was in fact ignorant, and much too nonchalant to think poorly of himself.

A Bug on a Bar-Room Wall

When it came down to making love, Roy could take it or leave it.

After this encounter 'neath the Naugahyde, the change in her whole sexual outlook and demeanor was hard to fathom. Earline was much younger and had boundless sexual energy. She was multi-orgasmic, and thought it was natural. Earline was not somewhat benign in her condition; she was malignantly pregnant from Roy's earlier input in the salad bowl. She was about to transmogrify in a manner never before witnessed in a cocktail lounge, ever.

The insurance lady asked the trucker if he had seen what she had seen. He had, (though there was no accounting for the tiny Roi-Tan cigar). The underwriter wanted to leave. The Karaoke music started. The juices flowed. They left. The trucker hummed; "My Way". There was a chill in the air under the cushion and outside of the lounge. The trucker was in his fifties.

"The Insurance Lady"

A Bug on a Bar-Room Wall

Around this time, several flights were taking to the air in different parts of the world. Master Sergeant Murray had slammed his fingers in a freak accident in a Hummer (or while getting a hummer). He was missing three, and headed from an Army base in Landstuhl, Germany to some therapy at Building 18, Walter Reed Hospital in Washington, DC. He still had his little roommates in his sea bag. They were safely ensconced in the belly of a Charter Lufthansa jet with all of the other cargo.

Jack Mac was staring out the window from his Jet Blue flight from JFK non- stop to San Diego. He had frostbite on two of his toes, and would probably lose them. This did not seem to affect his pool-shooting abilities, however so he had brought his pool stick case, along with his other worldly possessions, never to return to the snow. You know who was stowed away.

Johnny McGee was airborne for Seattle on flight 540, Alaska Airlines. He had earlier mobilized a project with tools and machinery with his dad, Willie, and was just making this short visit to touch up the project with finishing touches. He carried a tiny Samsonite suitcase and a small carry-on duffle containing a few paintbrushes and hand tools. They were renovating a medium sized hotel in Seattle near the waterfront. This project would continue for about five more months, so John planned to leave his brush bag in an unlit, abandoned hotel room. He did not know that it was humming with life.

Willie was at that point in his life where he was starting to feel comfortable with his lot. He stayed busy with his Beloved Polly and their small but successful business. To ward off insanity, he took to composing poetry and writing short stories. He had spent his life observing his wife rear their four wonderful offspring to certain points in their lives. Some of his notebooks might be worth reprinting here:

Bo Peep

Little Bo Peep has lost her sheep
And doesn't know where to find them.
Leave them alone and they will come home
Wagging their tails behind them.

Willie was thinking that on the surface the poem, or nursery rhyme, seems simple, a plain story of a little girl who has lost her sheep, but is anyone listening? This was significant to poor Willie. She has learned to leave them alone. Bo Peep is cool. She trusts her sheep. She does not go bothering them as they nibble away in pasture, glen, vale and hillside. They need their grass, their roughage, and the occasional draw of water from a tinkling little stream. Also, they have little lambs who need time for bonding with their mother after they have frolicked all day with their peers. They do not need the world barging in and destroying the mood. They might be sheep, they might be lambs, they might be ewes, they might be rams, but they are entitled to a little communal happiness before they are transformed into the mutton that the Irish consume, or the Cashmere that Willie wears.

His point was that perhaps people should stop bothering people. Little Bo Peep backs off. She could stay up all night, waiting and whimpering by the door. But she knows better. She trusts her sheep. She leaves them alone and they come home, and you can imagine the joyful reunion, a lot of merry bleating and grab-ass and deep expressions of satisfaction from the rams as they settle in for the night while Ms. Peep does her crossword by the fire happy in the knowledge that in her daily rounds, caring for sheep and their offspring, she has bothered nobody. As Mitch often says, "Live and let live".

Snow was appearing on Willies head and he had decided to enjoy the years left to him. He goes home.

Chapter Eleven
The Flowering Inferno

"Inferno"

Earline sensed that she was with child. Nature usually lets a mother know. She had a strange, new feeling in her underbelly, which was alien and not a little unnerving. The malady was at once physical and mental. Roy had all but ignored her and her condition. She had, by now resigned herself to a good riddance attitude. She mused that he was a hairy-legged dork and she could not imagine why she ever wanted him. She had reasoned correctly that she had been used and tossed like a used condom.

Her gestation period was of course two weeks, and she instinctively knew that it was time to locate her birthing place for her oncoming cockwiglets. Roy was of no assistance, a hideous caregiver and a genuine jerk. He seemed apathetic to her plight. Of course he asked about her health and made stupid comments about current events at *Naugahyde Hills*. She was nonplussed. She would nod at him and wave her feelers at him in disdain. It was as frigid in their lives as a train rail on a Chicago February morning. There was a perceptible chill in the air, which all males have experienced.

Earline squeezed in a few minutes to jot down some entries for Dina, her earwig mother. She related her journeys in various vehicles, and in threadbare pant cuffs. She described her exciting return in an empty mace holster. She narrated visions of living in a cardboard condominium, jockey shorts and a Naugahyde elbow cushion. She described dancing with Roy, dart games, the drunk tank and eavesdropping. She further informed her mother of the suicide and the general nature of owners and bartenders. She informed her mother that except for the nausea, life was indeed good.

She felt no further need for Roachmeister. He was jettisoned. Gone! She knew she had need for an immediate, secure sanctuary for her babies, which was unencumbered by the crush of human elbows. At last call, as the lights went up, the drunks got even homelier and the music died. The barroom became heavy with silence.

Earline eyed her perfect haven, the satellite tuner box. It was accessible, warm, and provided safety, since very few bartenders touched it and the owner did not know that it was there. The tuner was ideal, and beautifully furnished. It had

Zener diodes, microchips, Shockley diodes, resistors, capacitors, transistors, coils and LCDs. It was warm. This is my manger, she purred, and she did not need a Saint Joseph for help.

Her ova nestled softly in a mantle of pool table chalk and other dust. There was lint from nightly dancing and body twisting on the oaken dance floor. It was like a down pillow. This satellite tuner had not been opened since it was installed and was as safe a hideout as could be found in San Diego County.

Roy went about his business, betting over/under on football games and hanging with his homeboys under the slate of the pool table. His world was quite simple. Sleep in, hang out, make out, and sleep in. He was the only roach in the bar that smoked cigars. He was also the only one to wear shoes. In fact, he wore brown and white shoes on all of his feet. The white ones were often dirty. He was truly, as Earline had surmised, a great, hairy-legged dork. His nostrils were so large that he could pick his nose with his thumb. He was truly a mouth-breather from the waterfront.

Dr Seuss would have described Roy as a bad banana with a greasy black peel. His brain was full of spiders; his soul was full of funk. Roy was a three-decked sauerkraut and toadstool sandwich with arsenic sauce. Roy was loose and boneless. She was far better off without this guy in her life. What good are men?

A Bug on a Bar-Room Wall

Though the tungsten-haired Earline had no pretensions about how her future would unfold, she used absolute discretion in her thinking. She was anxious. She was irritable. She was alone and nervous. Her little heart was pounding at heartbreak speed. There was worry and insomnia. She had diarrhea. She was going to be a mom. She needed Dina. Four of her eggs hatched into the first cockwigs the world has seen.

Earline took some solace from the fact that her new home was warm. Since last call, the temperature had risen. It was really warm. In fact the temperature in her fuzzy nest had gone from the normal sixty degrees to an alarming one hundred eighty degrees Fahrenheit, perhaps too warm. The lint from a number of cheap sport coats and some Angora and Cashmere from sweaters had indeed become kindling. With the fluids in the transformers, the cockwig nest rose to a flash point, a flowering inferno. Fire!

The cockwigs scrambled after Earline. The box was ablaze. Her most formidable task in her life was at hand. Flames inside the home were licking at the anodized aluminum case of the Cox product. The wafer switches and other components were melting and incinerating. They knew true fear; as all of God's creatures know fear when flame appears.

The tangerine-colored flames licked at the Frazee oil-based enamel coating the adjacent wall. Plastic swizzle sticks erupted in a whoosh. Stacks of napkins exploded, further igniting the *Naugahyde Hills* community. Even the two-week-old Calla Lilly burst into flame. Her alarm was hard to describe. She instinctively knew that her first priority was to remove her offspring from any eminent danger or harm's way. She took a mental note and observed that their escape route should be to drop to the bar stools from atop *Naugahyde Hills* and wait for another option. Flame raged above them and smoke from toxic PVC plumbing covered the next stratum below. It was time to wait it out.

The Bar Owner had been testing his eyelids for pinholes with his feet propped upon his messy desk. He had been slumbering in his cramped and cluttered office, waiting for the effects of drinking his own booze to wear off. The acrid stench of burning plastic was annoying to his cratered, bulbous nose. He had thought he was dreaming and could not readily identify the crackling sounds as he attempted to unscrew his muddled mind. Fire!

He leapt to his feet and clumsily slipped into his ancient Salvation Army tasseled loafers, and scurried out to the blazing bar area to confront someone with anger at the situation. There was nobody to accost. He had all of the agility and coordination of a newborn baby. He noticed that one of the loafer tassels was missing, and thought about complaining to the Salvation Army Thrift Store. In his storeroom he heard one of Big Bird's forgotten boas burst into flame, as well as one of Gini's abandoned shawls.

To his horror, he finally realized that his establishment was engulfed in flame and toxic smoke, and was as dark as a yard up a chimney. He looked like a demented Jerry Colona in his big walrus moustache. Not having the pre-plan of a fire bill, he immediately picked up a telephone (for business only), and found that the phone was hot enough to singe the hair flowing from his right ear and to sear the calluses from his right hand. He then took his next logical step; unlock the entry door and scream for help. He quickly began placing his decrepit bar stools on the outside sidewalk, in a drizzling mist, where firemen might want to tread.

Even when his brain was in high gear, the owner still had a transmission problem. He gave no thought to saving his cash or any of his beloved, albeit watered- down hooch. All that he could seem to reckon was that his furniture had to be spared this holocaust. Sweat was streaming down his troubled countenance as he placed his final barstool next to a big red engine pumper. He had no earthly way of knowing that there, buried deeply in the excelsior seat padding, crouched Earline and her four little cockwigs.

The trusty fire department was there with their boots and bells on. They even woke the transient under the dumpster with their noise. The power went off, the water flew. It was like Coulee Dam overflowing. The flames had consumed vast quantities of Grand Marnier, VO, Gordon's Gin, and Spuds Mackenzie. A fifty-six Corvette scale model had gone to the eternal wrecking yard in the sky. The Juke Box had caved in and resembled a grotesque image of Al Davis. The battle lasted for twenty-three minutes and in the aftermath; the Olivetti cash register had vaporized into a puddle of melted coinage and crispy bundles of neatly sorted ash.

Our hapless owner stood in the dank, early morning mist with dirty tears streaming from his vermilion-colored eyes. It was nearly 0400 AM. He had no clue. The transient wanted a drink. His assets, including chits and bad checks were gone. His dance floor looked like Lake Murray with little oak tiles floating around, willy-nilly, amidst the Marlboro filters and tampons from the ladies room. It was like an overhead view of the Titanic with the flotsam and jetsam.

Nature is not really cruel. Nature is indifferent. In breeding and crossbreeding one must play by the rules of nature. It is a simple matter of natural selection all the way, survival of the fittest. Earline had one more ride coming. This time she would be accompanied by her covey of cockwigs. She had another tale to recount to her mother.

She cogitated and pondered how to describe her current journey. She reveled inside the darkness and safety of the tattered seat cushion. There was something familiar about this trip. It was the noise. She had heard that Detroit diesel whine before and in fact feared that she was returning to her roots at the Mesa Distributing Company in a beer truck. Not!

The trip ended. The roll-up door on the truck flew up. She saw the early morning daylight through a tear in the Naugahyde. There she observed a portly little man who rarely misses an opportunity to get something for nothing. She saw the balding pate and broad grin on the satisfied mug of Monsignor Joe Carroll of Saint Vincent de Paul. He does not miss a trick.

A Bug on a Bar-Room Wall

Afterbirth

In the year 2007, Cockwigs have been observed in places other than San Diego, California. Places such as Dublin, Ireland, New York, New York, Boston, Massachusetts and Kennebunkport, Maine. They have kinfolk in Baltimore, Maryland, Washington, D.C., Key West, Florida and New Orleans, Louisiana. Further generations of Cockwigs can be found in Dallas, Texas, Denver, Colorado, Lake Havasu, Peoria, Laughlin and Queen Creek, Arizona. Look for Cockwig aunts and uncles in Red Bluff, California, Bend, Oregon, White Center, Washington and Pearl City, Hawaii. Distant cousins reside in Yokosuka, Japan, where they are called Cockrigs. Throughout the world, bars are bars, people are people and bugs are bugs. We all get around, even with Homeland Security.

Author

Should you be so inclined to possess a copy of this experience for your own enjoyment send $11.25 to:

Willie McGee
3968 Park Boulevard
San Diego, California
92103

A Bug on a Bar-Room Wall

A Bug on a Bar-Room Wall

A Bug on a Bar-Room Wall